The Diary of Janie Ray

The Impossible Medallion

and

The Day My Mom Got Grounded!

By

Lila Segal

The Impossible Medallion

♥ March 3, 2011 ♥

Dear Diary,

Hi! My name is Janie Ray and I am eleven years old. I got this diary for my birthday last month and promised my mom (her name is Sheila) that I would write in it if she bought it for me. I am in fifth grade and believe it or not, my best friend is also named Sheila! Isn't that weird? She's really, really cool and we have tons of private jokes together. Like every time Mrs. Santini tells us to take out our math books, we totally crack up, because in the secret language we made up for our clubhouse, the letters m-a-t-h spell a really funny word. I'll tell you all about our language tomorrow.

Sheila has the best hair in our whole class and I am *so* jealous! She always complains about her hair, but I think she's crazy. It's long and straight and never sticks out. She thinks it's boring, but I would do *anything* to trade with her! My hair is incredibly thick and frizzy, and I usually wear it in a ponytail, because otherwise my mom says it's too messy.

Sheila has a huge crush on Calvin, who sits behind her in class. He's really cute. I think he likes her too, but she doesn't believe me, and she won't even sit next to him at lunch time.

I don't have a crush on anyone. I mean, I don't think boys are gross, but personally, I don't see why we have to get all googly eyed about them.

Oh my gosh, I have a huge math test tomorrow (m-a-t-h!!), so I have to go now. I did really badly on my last test, and my mom will be so mad if I don't study for this one.

Dear Diary,

URGH! I had my math test today, and it was horrible! We'll get our grades back next week, but I compared answers afterwards with Sheila, and I think I got at least three questions wrong. I seriously don't understand why we need to learn math. My dad (his name is Mark) says it will help me later on in life, but personally, I don't see why. I mean, it's not like I'm planning to be a mathematician or anything!

The rest of the day was pretty boring. At lunch, Marcia the Snob grabbed the piece of paper Sheila was doodling on and almost found out about her crush on Calvin! Sheila had drawn lots of little hearts with arrows through them and written "Sheila and Calvin" all over in pink magic marker. Lucky for her, she wrote it in our secret language, so MTS (Marcia the Snob, of course) had no idea what it said. That didn't stop her from jumping up and down, waving the paper around like a crazy person, and screeching, "Ooh, it looks like Sheila has a crush on *somebody*!" That MTS is such a pain!

Oh, I almost forgot! I promised to tell you about our secret language today. So here is the code (You just have to switch each letter of the regular alphabet with the secret letter underneath it):

A	B	C	D	E	F	G	H	I	J
o	h	r	m	I	q	n	k	e	p
K	**L**	**M**	**N**	**O**	**P**	**Q**	**R**	**S**	**T**
g	d	t	s	U	w	v	z	l	j
U	**V**	**W**	**X**	**Y**	**Z**				
a	x	f	b	Y	c				

My name in code is "POSEI" and Sheila's is "LKIEDO". So instead of Sheila and Calvin, her note said "LKIEDO OSM RODXES".

TJL EL O WOES!!!!

(Oh, and in case you haven't figured it out yet, m-a-t-h spells DUMB! Coincidence? I think not.)

♥ March 8, 2011 ♥

Dear Diary,

Today was the worst. The absolute pits.

It started out o.k. – I got up on time to have breakfast and even made it to school a few minutes early. It always makes my mom very happy when I have breakfast. She says it's the most important meal of the day and loves making us pancakes and French toast and stuff, even though she only ever has coffee herself.

I think parents like to see their kids eat. I don't really get it, though. They seem to spend all their time trying to get us to eat *more*, while they're busy trying to eat *less* themselves. Every time we have a big meal, my dad complains that he ate too much and my mom unbuttons her pants and says she feels "fat". But if we don't eat everything on *our* plates, they tell us we should finish up so that we can join the "Clean Plate Club". When I was little, I actually thought there was a club like that, and that if I ate all my food I would get to join.

Go figure. Grown-ups sure are weird sometimes.

The first couple of hours at school weren't too bad, either. During English class, I got to switch seats with Jessica. Mrs. Santini made her move, because she couldn't stop talking to her friend Alexis. And I'm really happy about it, since it means I don't have to sit next to Ben White anymore. Ben *really* gets on my nerves. He always puts his elbows on my side of the table, and when I ask him to move over, he just grunts and moves like one inch. He's the kind of kid who brings five sharpened pencils to every test, even though he never breaks any of them. And he always knows the answers in math class. Once my pencil broke during a history test, and there he was, with all those pencils laid out on the desk next to him. But would he let me borrow one? No! Isn't that just the most obnoxious thing ever?? No offense, but that is such a *boy* thing to do.

Anyway, I got to move and sit next to Alexis. She's a pretty nice kid, even though she's friends with MTS. She has this thing about Angry Birds, and all her things – her notebooks, her pencil case, and even her erasers – are covered with them. Go figure. And she's really into sports. Her mom always packs her amazing lunches, with stuff I would never be allowed to have – like peanut butter and Marshmallow Fluff sandwiches – and she's usually willing to share her food with people.

Anyway, it was after that that everything started going downhill. First, MTS and her friends all started giggling when they saw me in the hallway during recess. I have no idea why. They are such banana brains! Then, in math class, I got my test back and got a lousy 78. I think Sheila did better than me, but I'm not really sure, because she never tells anyone her grades. Her mom says grades are private. In general, though, she does pretty well in school.

At lunch, I tripped on my shoelaces and dropped my tray all over the floor, and some of my pudding landed on Calvin's shoes! He was really nice about it, but Sheila said she almost died.

But the most horrible part was when I got home in the afternoon. I caught SRJ (Silly RJ, of course) in my room, playing with my (new, amazing, totally-off-limits-to-RJ) tablet! I shrieked at the top of my lungs, and my mom came rushing in to see what happened. But of course, instead of yelling at SRJ, she yelled at *me* and told me I was setting a bad example for him. A bad example!? He was the one cackling like a wild hyena just to make me mad. SRJ *always* goes into my room and touches my stuff, and my parents never get mad at him, because they say he's only four years old and doesn't know any better. It's so unfair! When I was four, they never let *me* get away with anything. I had to clean my room practically every day, and his room is always a huge mess. I'm officially not speaking to my mom.

Dear Diary,

Turns out yesterday was only the *second* worst day of my life. When I got to school this morning, I found out what MTS and her dumb friends had been giggling about. As soon as I walked into the classroom, everyone suddenly got quiet, and I saw a huge picture of a lion taped to the front of my desk with the words "JANIE the FRIZZ" scribbled underneath! MTS and her lousy gang were all standing by the blackboard, covering their mouths with their hands and looking at the floor, and I just knew they had something to do with it. I ran out of the room and hid in the bathroom crying, until Sheila came looking for me after first recess (she had a dentist's appointment this morning). I've never been so humiliated in my entire life!

All day long, people roared at me and made stupid lion comments when they saw me in the hall. Why does MTS have to be so mean? What did I ever do to her?

The worst part is, I think MTS must have overheard my mom reminding me at drop off the other day to wear my scrunchie, so that my hair wouldn't frizz!

Now I'm doubly not speaking to my mom. She always looks so nice and everything is always so easy for her! I'll bet *she* never got made fun of at school.

♥ March 12, 2011 ♥

Dear Diary,

Today is Saturday and it's raining out. Sheila and I were supposed to go play kickball in the park this morning, but the field is all muddy and the game was cancelled.

Things with my mom are really weird. At breakfast this morning she made us pancakes with chocolate chips *and* French toast, and she even gave me hot apple cider with a cinnamon stick. I didn't tell her about what happened at school last week, but I guess she can tell I'm pretty mad about *something*. I tried to keep up not speaking to her, but by the end of breakfast I kind of laughed at some of her jokes and let her give me a hug. But I'm still mad!

She told me that when she was my age, she used to get angry at *her* mom for taking her sister's side and yelling at her when they fought. I'm not sure I believe her, though. I can't even imagine my mom fighting with Auntie Karen. I'll bet she was Little Miss Perfect when she was eleven!

Dear Diary,

You are seriously not going to believe what happened to me this morning. I was cleaning my room and came across this old medallion I found when I was seven, on our vacation in Miami. It's really neat – shiny, black, round and smooth - and it has a really weird inscription on it:

Posei: Kudm jenkjdy osm loy jki moji a fosj ju xelej jkzii jetil

It's been sitting in my jewelry box for years, and when I saw it yesterday, I suddenly noticed something incredible: *The first word of the inscription, which never made any sense to me, spells my name in the secret language I made up with Sheila!*

That got me thinking, and I decided to see what would happen if I plugged our code into the rest of the inscription, just for the heck of it. And this is the unbelievable part, the part that doesn't make any sense. Turns out the inscription says:

Janie: hold tightly and say the date u want to visit three times

If I hadn't seen that medallion and its crazy inscription with my own two eyes, years before Sheila and I ever even made up our code, I'd figure it was MTS trying to play some kind of a trick on me or something. So I don't blame you if you think I'm nuts. I would too, if I were you. It's impossible!!!

Naturally, I called Sheila right away, and she nearly choked on her cucumber sticks when she saw it. Luckily, she's seen the medallion before, so she knows I'm not making it up.

"Hold tightly and say the date you want to visit three times"? What in heck could that mean? How could something have been written in our secret language *four years* before we even made it up? And how in the world am I supposed to concentrate on my English homework tonight?

Sheila and I are having a special meeting in our clubhouse tomorrow after school to talk about this mystery and try and figure things out. Meanwhile, I gotta go – my mom wants me to come down for dinner, and I have to hide the medallion so that SRJ doesn't find it.

♥ March 14, 2011 ♥

Dear Diary,

If you thought I was nuts yesterday, you're really going to freak out today. This whole medallion thing keeps getting weirder and weirder!

This morning I could barely concentrate on anything at school, even in English class. Mrs. Moore called on me three times and yelled at me for not knowing what page they were on. On the bright side, I nearly forgot about the whole lion business, and it seems like most of the kids in the class have forgotten about it too. Except for MTS & Company, that is.

Right after school, Sheila and I ran home as fast as we could, grabbed a snack and went out to the clubhouse to talk about *the situation*. What happened next took us both by surprise, and even though it's still today (or at least, I hope it is), so much has happened, and I'll just have to tell you the story...

******

"I don't know, Janie," Sheila said uncertainly, bouncing a rubber ball against the clubhouse wall. "There has to be a reasonable explanation for this. Maybe this is a *different* medallion than the one you found when you were seven. Maybe MTS or someone figured out how to switch the medallion you had with a new one. Nothing else makes any sense!"

"I know," I answered. "But first of all, MTS doesn't even know our language, and she's never been in my room! And second, I specifically remember the medallion having a strange inscription on it when I found it."

"Well," she said, thoughtfully chewing a hangnail off her pinky. "I've always wondered how I would react if something unbelievable happened. Like if someone had special powers or something and managed to prove they could lift things with their eyes or read people's thoughts. I've always wondered whether I'd believe them or not, or whether I'd be too scared to accept the possibility that things we don't believe in might actually be true. This is kind of like that, right?"

"What do you mean?"

"Well, here we have a situation where something seemingly impossible has happened, and we can't explain it any other way. I don't know, maybe we should just accept that something unusual really *is* going on."

"Ok," I said, picking up the medallion and turning it over in my hands. "Let's say we *do* accept that we don't know what's going on. What should we do?"

There was quiet as we each considered my words.

"Well," Sheila finally said, grinning mischievously. "Maybe we should just do what it says."

"Huh?" I said, startled.

"Maybe we should do what it says," Sheila repeated quietly. "Hold it tightly and say the date we want to visit three times."

"What, you mean – time travel?" My eyes widened.

"I guess," she answered. "Or at least, I think that's what I mean."

"Well, where should we go?" I asked. "Or rather, *when* should we go?

We both giggled excitedly. Sheila wrinkled her brow before suddenly grabbing my hand, grasping it together with the medallion, and blurting out, "July 5, 1739! July 5, 1739! July 5, 1739!"

******

Holy cow. Geez Louis. Yikes!!!

After Sheila grabbed my hand, everything went haywire. We plunged down into a dark tunnel and fell, shrieking our heads off, for what seemed like forever. It was kind of like being in an elevator that's going down super fast, making you feel like your tummy is about to fly up into your nose and your head is going to explode.

Then we landed with a *thump* in a small, rocky clearing, surrounded by trees as far as the eye could see.

Sheila got up first, brushed herself off, and looked around. "Where the heck are we?"

I rubbed my eyes and stood up slowly. "I-I don't know," I said quietly, trying not to panic. My trembling voice was drowned out by a loud noise behind me, and I whirled around to see a huge pine tree swaying back and forth and looking like it was about to fall over.

"Watch out!" I yelled, shoving Sheila out of the way. I pushed her onto the ground and landed in a heap on top of her.

"Hey, what are you -" she started to protest. But then she grew silent, a stunned look on her face, as the humongous tree toppled over and crashed

about two feet away from us. It was so big that it made the ground shake.

We sat there speechless for several seconds, and I pinched myself to make sure I wasn't dreaming. *This seriously could* **not** *be happening.*

I turned to Sheila and opened my mouth to speak, but before I could say anything, I saw something out of the corner of my eye that shocked me back into silence. A huge man with really strange clothes was walking towards us, looking very angry.

And worst of all, he was carrying an axe!

"Who is there?" he thundered. He was speaking English, but I couldn't place his accent. As he got nearer, I could see he looked about my dad's age, and his face – which was kindly, despite his anger - took on a concerned expression. "What are you two girls doing on my property? And why are you unattended! Are you hurt? I am chopping wood here today! And I am sure I do not have to tell you how perilous that can be!" He peered down at us and furrowed his brow. "What are you girls wearing? Where are you from?"

Sheila and I glanced at each other, and then, as if by unspoken agreement, we both scrambled to our feet and started running away as fast as we could. We must have taken the man by surprise, because he just stood there, his mouth open, and watched us go.

We ran and ran for what seemed like hours, but was probably more like ten minutes, before Sheila stopped and leaned against a tree.

"Wait," she said between breaths. "I need my inhaler." Sheila has asthma, and always carries a small, white inhaler with her in her pocket.

"Ok." I looked around, catching my breath, and was relieved to see no one had followed us. We were in the middle of a forest, with pine trees all around, and in the distance I could hear the faint sound of running water. A creek? I reached up to brush a few stray strands of hair out of my eyes. My head was hot and sweaty, and my hair felt even frizzier than usual. It must have been close to ninety degrees out! *Not March weather at all,* I thought. I pinched myself again, wondering if maybe I was just losing my mind.

"Wow." Sheila broke into my thoughts. "T-t-this is u-unbelievable! D-do you think we really t-travelled through time?" She had an awed look on her face as she stuffed the inhaler back in her pocket.

"I don't know..." my voice trailed off.

"Well, t-that guy sure didn't look like he lived in the twenty-first century." Sheila managed a weak smile.

I nodded mutely. That was for sure.

"So what should we do now?" Sheila moved a couple of rocks out of her way and sat down on the ground, suddenly all business. "Let's make a plan. You still have the medallion, right?" That's one great thing about Sheila - she can be pretty impulsive sometimes, but she's a very practical person.

My heart skipped a beat, and I reached into my pocket, breathing a sigh of relief when I felt the cool medallion against the palm of my hand. "Yup, it's here." I sat down next to her.

"Ok, so the way I see it, we have two options. We can stay here and explore a bit or -"

I shook my head vigorously. "No way. We need to get out of here right away! We don't even know where - or when! - we are!"

Sheila giggled. "Sure we do! We're in 1739."

I shook my head again. "Just because you said 1739, that doesn't mean that's where we are. We don't even know how this medallion works!" Then I stopped. "Wait a minute. Why did you choose 1739, anyway?"

Sheila giggled again. "I don't know, I just thought it would be cool to see all that stuff we're learning about in history class. Like the Boston Tea Party."

I rolled my eyes. Sheila might be better than me in math, but history was my favorite subject. "The Boston Tea Party happened in 1773, genius. We just learned about that two days ago! And anyway, it happened in *Boston*." I gestured to the trees around us. "We could be in Timbuktu for all we know."

Sheila gave me a sheepish smile. "Well, I was close," she said.

Just then, I heard another loud noise coming from behind Sheila, and looked up to see a horse galloping in our direction. "Watch out!" I yelled for the second time at the top of my lungs, rolling aside and pulling Sheila with me. I buried my face in my hands and waited for the horse to go by, praying it wouldn't trample us. A few seconds passed, and I heard a loud whinnying. Then someone said "Whoa boy!" and the galloping came to a slow halt. When I finally picked up my head, I saw a young girl about our age, standing over us with her hands on her hips. She was short and thin, and was wearing a dark brown dress with what looked like a white apron over it. Her hair was pulled back into a neat braid, partially covered with a gleaming white bonnet, but her dress was incredibly dirty and one of her sleeves had a big hole in it.

"Who are you?" she demanded, shifting her weight from one side to the other. Her horse, which she had already managed to tie to a nearby tree, whinnied loudly again. "Quiet!" she said, swatting it with a small stick she picked up from the ground.

Sheila and I just sat there, and I opened my mouth, but the words were stuck in my throat.

"I said, who are you?" she demanded again. Then her eyes narrowed. "Are you boys or girls?"

That seemed to break the spell, and Sheila jumped up and faced the girl indignantly. "Hey, what is that supposed to mean?"

The girl took a step back, surprised, and stared at us for several moments. "I apologize," she said finally. "I can see you are girls. But I have never seen girls wearing pants before! And I am not sure what hay has to do with anything!" Then she grinned and gestured to the horse. "I like girls who are not afraid to do what boys do. My parents hate it when I ride George. They say a *little lady* like me should not go horseback riding alone." She said the words *little lady* in a mimicking tone, and then wrinkled her nose and snorted. "But I think they are just old-fashioned!" She stuck out her hand. "My name is Penelope. What are your names?"

Sheila reached out and shook her hand. "My name is Sheila!" she said. "And this is Janie." She helped me up and I stood slowly, brushing the pine needles off my jeans.

"Nice to meet you!" Penelope said. "Where are you from? You do not look like you are from here."

Sheila and I met each other's eyes. "No, we aren't from here. We're kind of - lost." I managed.

The girl gave me a funny look. "You have an odd way of speaking," she said. "Well, maybe I can help you find your way. Where are you trying to go?"

"Boston!" Sheila blurted out, before I had a chance to reply. I shot her a look.

The girl's eyes widened. "Boston? That is almost 700 miles away from here! Even if you had a horse and carriage, it would take you more than two weeks to get there!"

"Uh, where are we?" I asked. I didn't dare ask her *when* we were. She already thought we were complete lunatics.

The girl looked at me strangely again. "We are in Edenton, North Carolina, of course." *Edenton, North Carolina?!* A chill went down my spine.

Then she pointed off in the distance. "I live over there. I cannot take you to Boston, but I am certain my parents would not mind having guests for supper. They are going to be furious when they see what I have done to my dress." She pointed at the hole in her sleeve and winked at us. "But they may not scold me as much if there is company. My house is just one mile away. You will come with me."

It was a statement, not a question. I looked at Sheila, and was surprised to see her nodding eagerly.

"Uh, that's very kind of you," I said to Penelope. "I just need to talk to my friend in private for a minute." I grabbed Sheila's elbow and pulled her aside.

Penelope sniffed. "Do you not know it is rude to share secrets when others are around?" She turned and started walking slowly towards her horse, shaking her head. "I will wait for you over here."

As she walked away, I turned to face Sheila. "Are you insane?" I whispered. "We can't go with her. We have to get out of here!"

"Why?" Sheila asked, and I could tell by the gleam in her eye that it was no use trying to convince her. "We have the medallion. If anything happens, we can just use it to go home." She put her hand on my shoulder. "Please, Janie? Just think how much fun it'll be! And what if we really are in 1739? That would be the coolest thing EVER!"

I took a deep breath. She did have a point. If we could use the medallion to get home, there would be no harm in waiting a little while and exploring a bit. And if we were going to stay here, going to Penelope's house made more sense than trying to find our way all alone in the forest. Especially since we didn't have water or food or anything. At the thought of food, my stomach growled, and it occurred to me I hadn't eaten anything but a little snack since lunchtime. I reached into my pocket and fingered the medallion. "Ok," I said finally. "Let's go - but only for a short time!"

Sheila gave me a quick hug and squealed with excitement. "This is going to be EPIC!!"

******

We followed Penelope in the direction of her house, silently trudging through the forest. Except for the sound of branches and leaves crackling under our feet, and a few birds chirping in the distance, everything seemed oddly quiet. I nudged Sheila in the ribs and whispered in her ear, "Do you hear that?"

"Hear what?"

"Exactly. There are no cars or trucks or anything!"

Sheila stopped and listened for a few seconds before nodding. "Yeah, it's pretty creepy."

We continued walking in an awkward silence for another twenty minutes or so, before arriving at a small, two-story white house with wooden panels and a large yard closed off by a yellow fence. "This is my house!" Penelope said proudly, tying her horse to a tree. Then she faced us, lowering her voice and speaking quickly. "There is an elderly woman who lives in our town and keeps to herself. Her name is Emily Hodgson. If my parents ask you where you are from, tell them that she is your grandmother, and that you are visiting her for the summer from Virginia. They never speak to her, so they will not discover the truth. And do not tell them your real names." She pointed at Sheila. "You will be Patience." Then she pointed at me. "And you will be Modesty."

Sheila stifled a giggle, and I frowned. It would so *figure* that I would get the really weird name.

"Um, ok." I said, brushing away the uneasy feeling that was starting to form in the pit of my stomach. *And what if they didn't believe us?*

"No, wait a minute." Penelope was looking us up and down and shaking her head. "This will not do at all. Your clothes are too odd, and my parents will be suspicious. Wait here."

Before we could protest, she raced to the side of the house and started climbing up a large oak tree that was almost touching an upstairs window. She opened it and tumbled inside, emerging a few seconds later with something wrapped around her shoulders.

"She's quite the little lady," Sheila said with a wry grin. I smiled in spite of myself.

Penelope ran back in our direction and shoved two dresses with matching bonnets at us. "Go behind that tree and put these on. I shall hide your things."

We did what she said, and I breathed a sigh of relief when the dress slid easily onto me. I was at least two sizes taller than Penelope, but the dress seemed to be a one-size-fits-all kind of thing, with strings you could pull to adjust the width. It was a little short on me, but not too bad.

As Penelope opened the door to her house, a tall, plump woman with a tight, graying bun in her hair walked up and took her by the arm. She looked pretty mad. "Penelope Padgett! Why, I never saw a young lady as filthy as you are today! Go right upstairs and -" She stopped abruptly and stared at us.

"Who -"

"These are my new friends, Mamma! Patience and Modesty," Penelope said quickly. "They are visiting their grandmother from Virginia and I would like to invite them to join us for supper!"

The woman stood up straight and eyed us suspiciously. I kicked myself. I should have taken off my scrunchie! They probably didn't have *those* in 1739. We must have passed some kind of a test though, because her face softened. "Of course they may stay," she said to Penelope. "But you *must* go upstairs and change your clothes. I hope you were not riding that awful horse again!"

"Ok, Mamma." Penelope muttered. "Come, girls, you may wait with me in my room."

I glanced around as we climbed up the stairs, taking in our surroundings. The house definitely looked old-fashioned, and it suddenly struck me that there were no light switches on any of the walls. The wooden floor was bare, with no carpeting, and the paint on the walls was peeling.

But it was as we followed Penelope down a long hallway to her room, that I saw something that nearly knocked my socks off. On a small decorative table that stood by her door lay a newspaper called the "South Carolina Gazette". And under the name of the paper, in unmistakable print, was the date: July 5th, 1739. I shivered and wrapped my arms around my chest. *This doesn't make any sense,* I thought, putting my hand on the table to steady myself as a wave of dizziness washed over me. *People don't just travel through time!*

Penelope's room didn't look that much different from the rest of the house. There was a simple single bed in the corner, a small closet, and a place for candles. Several pieces of clothing were strewn about on the floor. I nudged Sheila. "I guess she doesn't have a TV in her room, huh."

Sheila giggled softly. "I guess not."

Penelope gestured for us to sit down on her bed, and began pulling off her dress without even asking us to look away. I tried not to stare, but I couldn't help stealing curious glances, and it soon became clear why she didn't mind changing in front of two perfect strangers - she was wearing more clothes under her dress than most people wear at all! She threw the dirty dress on the floor and rummaged around in her closet for a clean one.

Sheila tapped me on the shoulder and winked. "I didn't know they had messy rooms in the olden days," she whispered.

"What?" Penelope said, looking at Sheila with a furrowed brow. "What did you say?"

"Oh - I, uh, just," Sheila stammered. "I was just telling Janie that I also have a messy room."

"Messy? Oh, you mean disorderly." Penelope smiled. "Yes, my mother always wants me to put everything away just so, but I cannot be bothered. She spends all her time cleaning the house, and never does anything fun!"

My eyes wandered to the window, and I saw two girls sitting outside, weaving something on a large loom, like the ones I had seen when I visited Colonial Williamsburg with my parents last year. It looked like something out of a movie set.

Penelope must have noticed me staring, because then she said, "Those are my two sisters, Elizabeth and Sarah. Do you have any brothers or sisters?"

"Yeah, I have a little brother," I said. "He's kind of a pain."

"A pain?" Penelope furrowed her brow again. "You mean he is ill?"

I winced. "No, I just mean - He can be a little bit annoying sometimes."

Penelope looked relieved. "Yes, I know what you mean. My older sister Elizabeth is such a goody two-shoes! She always does exactly what Mamma tells her, and she dresses nicely every day. My sisters share a room, and it is always in perfect order! Sometimes I cannot stand them."

Then I had an idea. "Hey, would it be ok if I took a look at the newspaper on the table over there?" I asked.

"What?" Penelope turned to look at me, both eyebrows raised. "You mean the South Carolina Gazette? You know how to read?"

"I, um, I -" I stuttered and looked helplessly at Sheila. *What was the right answer?*

"Yes, our fathers taught us both to read," Sheila rescued me. "They, um, think it is important for girls to get an education."

Penelope sighed and walked over to the door, returning with the newspaper. "You are very lucky. I have been trying to teach myself to read these past few months, but it is still very hard for me."

"You mean, you don't have to go to school?" I asked.

She shook her head. "No, there is no school in this area."

Just then we heard a harried voice calling from downstairs, "Penelope! It is almost time for supper! Please set the table right away! Why must I ask you again?"

"Ok, Mamma!" Penelope called back. She motioned for us to follow her. "Come, it is time to eat."

After Penelope left the room, Sheila quickly ripped off the front page of the paper and stuffed it into her apron pocket. I raised my eyebrows at her, and she grinned. "Just a little souvenir. You know, for history class."

******

We helped Penelope set the table with large wooden plates and spoons, and as I was putting the last plate down on the table, the door opened and a tall man walked in. When I saw his face, my blood ran cold and I grabbed Sheila by the arm.

"Ouch!" she said, pulling away from me.

"It's him!" I whispered.

"What?"

"Don't look now, but the man who just came in is the guy with the axe! I guess he must be her father!"

Sheila looked up automatically and gasped.

"I said, don't look!"

"Well, what should we do?" Sheila's forehead was creased with worry.

"I don't know. Maybe we should go back home now." I reached for my pocket and nearly fainted as my hand felt the stiff fabric of the dress Penelope had given me. *I wasn't wearing my own clothes anymore, and the medallion was still in my jeans pocket!!* My mouth went dry and I swallowed hard, trying desperately to think back to what Penelope had said when she gave us the clothes. *Where had she said she had hidden our stuff?*

37

Keeping my face turned to the side, I came up behind Penelope and asked quietly, "Um, where did you put my clothes?" I tried to keep my voice nonchalant.

Penelope smiled. "Do not worry, your things are in a safe place. I will show you later."

I hesitated. If I pressed her, she might get suspicious and want to see for herself why I needed my clothes so badly. But how long could we keep this up without her dad realizing that we were the strange kids he had seen in the forest?

I pulled Sheila into the next room and explained the situation. "I don't think we have a choice. We'll have to wait until after supper to get the medallion back. And maybe he won't recognize us. He only saw us for a few seconds, and we were wearing different clothes!"

We walked back into the kitchen, where the family had already begun assembling around the table. The man had taken his place at the head of the table, and Penelope's mom was sitting across from him at the other end. Penelope motioned for us to sit down next to her.

"Modesty, perhaps you would like to say grace?" Penelope's father had an expectant look on his face, and it took me a few seconds to realize he was talking to me.

"Um, I -" *Now what?*

The family was holding hands around the table, so I took Penelope and Sheila's hands in mine and squeezed them, trying to conjure up the blessings I had learned in Sunday school. Finally I managed, "Um, Thank you, Lord, for this food and, um, bless the hands that prepared it."

That seemed to do the trick, because they all answered "Amen", picked up their spoons and began to eat. Sheila caught my eye and winked at me. "Way to go!" she mouthed silently.

I took a tentative bite of the pudding and bread Penelope's mom put on the table, mentally preparing myself to just chew and swallow, no matter how bad it was. I'm not the pickiest eater in the world - at least not compared to RJ - but I'm not one of those kids that likes everything, either. Hmm. It was actually kind of good! I heard loud slurping noises next to me and cast a glance at Sheila, who was busy gulping down her food, attracting strange looks from Penelope's sisters.

"So, where are you girls from?" Penelope's father had put his spoon down and was eyeing us strangely.

"Um, we're from Virginia," Sheila replied. "We're here visiting our grandmother, Emily Hodgson."

Wow, she was good.

"Emily Hodgson? I did not know she had grandchildren." Penelope's father looked thoughtful. "She is such a quiet and strange old woman. You know," he added after a pause, "many people have wondered whether she is a witch."

"Samuel!" Penelope's mother chided him. "What a terrible thing to say. I am quite certain that their grandmother is a perfectly nice lady!" She turned to us. "Where are you from in Virginia, dears?"

Where in Virginia? "Um, Williamsburg?" I said. That was the first place that popped into my mind. I crossed my fingers, hoping they didn't know too many people there.

"Ah, Williamsburg is a fine place." Penelope's father let out a large belch. "Elizabeth, dear, you have prepared a wonderful supper. Now I must go, I have patients to attend to." He stood up and left the table, patting his eldest daughter on the head.

Penelope stood up too. "I shall take my friends back to their grandmother's house now," she said, motioning for us to follow.

"Thank you so much for a delicious meal," Sheila said, pushing her chair back and standing up.

"Yes, we are, uh, very grateful for your kindness," I added. It was funny how we were starting to talk so formally after being there for just a couple of hours.

Once outside, Penelope led us through a grassy field and into a small barn that looked like it was falling apart. The sun was setting, and it was already getting dark. "You shall sleep here," she pronounced. "And in the morning we will make a plan to get you back home." She seemed to have assumed we were actually *from* Boston, and I certainly wasn't about to correct her.

"Um, ok... But Penelope, where are our things?" I made a huge effort to keep the panic out of my voice.

She rolled her eyes. "I told you already that you do not need to worry. I have put them in a safe place, and I will give them back to you in the morning. It is better that they remain hidden until you leave."

Sheila and I exchanged worried glances. How had we let this happen? We were at this girl's mercy now, and we just had to pray she didn't go through our stuff or try and keep us here.

"Now go to sleep," she said firmly, walking towards the door of the barn. "I will come and wake you before dawn. Good night!"

As the door swung shut behind Penelope, Sheila and I slumped down on the piles of hay we were supposed to sleep on and I scowled at her.

"What?" she said, defensively.

"If you hadn't insisted on staying here, we wouldn't be in this mess. Who knows what she's gonna do with our stuff. We might be stuck here forever!" I lay down on my back and closed my eyes.

Sheila just sat there, pushing hay around with her foot and chewing glumly on a fingernail. "I'm sorry," she said quietly. "You're right."

Somehow, hearing her admit she was wrong didn't feel quite as good as I thought it would. I sat up and put my hand on her shoulder. "Well, I guess it's not really your fault. I agreed to stay too! And I'm the one who left the medallion in my stupid jeans pocket."

Sheila smiled at me gratefully. "Whoever's fault it is, we have to get our stuff back and get the heck out of here! I say we get a few hours' sleep, and then as soon as Penelope wakes us in the morning, we grab our clothes and make a run for it."

"Sounds like a plan."

******

My eyes started to close the moment my head hit the pile of hay I was using for a pillow, and the next thing I knew, I awoke with a start. I could have sworn it was just a few minutes later, but a faint light had already begun peeking in through the cracks in the barn. I rubbed my eyes, reached over and tapped Sheila on the shoulder. "Um, do you have any idea what they do around here for bathrooms?"

Sheila grunted and turned over, pulling the thin blanket we had been using over her head. "No idea," she mumbled. "Maybe you should just find a tree or something."

Ugh. Have I mentioned I *hate* going to the bathroom in nature?

I rolled off the pile of hay and quietly tiptoed outside, looking for a place to do my business. And that's when I heard the footsteps. Someone was coming! I slipped behind the nearest tree and craned my neck to listen, my heart racing. I heard the creak of the barn door swinging open and then a female voice that sounded like Penelope's mother:

"Where are you really from?"

There was a muffled reply, and then what sounded like a male voice:

"It was only after I fell asleep that I realized that you are the girls I saw in the forest yesterday, wearing those strange clothes. Emily Hodgson is not really your grandmother, is she? We shall pay Mrs. Hodgson a visit, right now! Where is your sister? If that is really what she is!"

I held my breath, frantically going over my options in my mind. *Calm down, Janie,* I told myself, *think!* I could run out and join Sheila, who was probably terrified, but then what about the medallion? There had to be a way to -

The footsteps were getting closer again, and I heard Sheila say loudly, "She's not here! She went home to our grandma's house!" It seemed like Sheila was trying to send me a message, and I suddenly realized what I had to do.

I waited until the footsteps had faded and took a few tentative steps out from behind the tree. In the distance, I could see Penelope's parents getting into a carriage with Sheila and I ran as fast as I could to the front door of the house. I tried the handle, and a knot formed in the pit of my stomach when it wouldn't turn. Of course it wouldn't. It was locked.

I turned and ran around to the side of the house, and when I reached the big oak tree outside Penelope's window, I stopped and took in several deep breaths.

Let's just say climbing trees is not exactly my favorite thing in the world. It's not that I'm afraid of heights. It's more like - I'm afraid of falling.

I closed my eyes and grabbed the first branch. It was surprisingly easy to pull myself up, and just a few seconds later I was outside Penelope's window. *Whatever you do, don't look down*, I told myself firmly. The window was just a few inches from the tree, but my heart stopped as I reached out and held onto the window sill. Luckily, the window was open halfway and there was enough room for me to jump through it. I counted to ten. *Here goes nothing.*

I landed hard on Penelope's floor and picked myself up, stifling a yelp as I stubbed my toe on the side of her bed. She was snoring softly, not a care in the world, and I felt like throttling her.

"Penelope, wake up!" I whispered urgently. When she didn't respond, I reached out and shook her gently.

Finally she sat up, confused. "Who - What – What is going on?" She saw me and gave a little jump, and then she must have remembered who I was, because she calmed down a little and lay back on her pillow.

"What is going on, Modesty?" she said sleepily. "I mean, Janie."

"Penelope! It's an emergency! Your parents came down to the barn and found Sheila! They know we're not Emily Hodgson's granddaughters, and they're taking her there right now!"

Penelope sat up again abruptly. "What?" she said. Her face had gone pale. "Then why are you here? Why did they not take you with them?"

I flushed. "I was outside, um, you know -"

She nodded.

"Well, we don't have any time to lose! You must give me my things right away, and we must go after them!"

Penelope nodded again. "Yes, if my parents find out that I fibbed to them, I will be punished very severely! Let us go right away!"

I looked at her and shook my head. Was her stupid punishment all she cared about? What about us?

She climbed out of bed and yawned, reaching for her bathrobe. She was moving *way* too slowly. *You're killing me, Penelope*, I thought. *Can't you go any faster?* She was one stubborn girl, that was for sure.

46

"Um, do you think you could hurry it up a bit?" I finally said.

"I am going as fast as I can!" She yawned again. But she threw on her dress and pulled a pile of things out from under her bed, pushing them in my direction. "Here are your clothes."

I glanced around for a place to change, and realized I'd have to do it right where I was. I pulled on my jeans under my dress and thrust my hand into the pocket, breathing only once my hand felt the cool, smooth medallion. I was flooded with relief. We could do this.

I quickly put on my shirt and handed the dress back to Penelope. Then, as I rolled Sheila's clothes up into a bundle, something heavy dropped to the floor. Her cellphone! I reached down and scooped it up quickly, stuffing it into my pocket and hoping desperately that Penelope hadn't noticed. Granted, it would be pretty interesting to see what Miss Penelope had to say about *that*, but we really didn't have any time for games.

We raced down the stairs and Penelope shouted back at me, "We will ride George together. Maybe if we get there before my parents, we can convince the crazy, old lady to tell them she is your grandmother. You know, she probably *is* a witch."

I gulped. I'd been to horseback riding camp a few times, but we only ever walked or trotted - we never galloped, and we ALWAYS wore proper riding gear. I had a feeling being careful wasn't Penelope's strong point.

I climbed gingerly onto the horse behind Penelope, and she turned and grinned at me mischievously. "I hope you are ready." And then, without even waiting for my reply she shouted "Giddy up!" and pulled the horse's reins. I braced myself, closing my eyes tightly and clutching on to her waist so hard my fingers started to hurt. But then, as we gained speed, I began to relax. This was actually kind of fun. I had no choice to but to trust Penelope, and it was a good feeling to finally let go for a few minutes.

I smiled as the cool wind blew my hair back out of my face, and I turned my head slightly to watch the scenery that raced by. There were lots of farmhouses and *tons* of animals, and in the distance I could even see the edges of the forest we had first arrived in.

We rode in silence, and about fifteen minutes later we started slowing down in front of a large, dark house with broken shutters and a red fence that looked sorely in need of repair. I drew in a sharp breath. Penelope's parents' carriage was parked in front of the house. We hadn't beaten them, after all.

We climbed off the horse, and Penelope motioned for me to follow her, placing a finger over her lips. "We must find a place to tie him up," she whispered. As we made our way quietly around to the back of the house, I tried desperately to come up with a plan. Should I just walk in, grab Sheila and use the medallion in front of everyone? Or should I try and play it cool?

Penelope found a place for George and then crouched under a large open window. "I can hear them," she whispered.

I crouched down next to her and could just barely make out the voice of a man coming from inside the house. "So of course, we thought it best to come right over here and find out if their story was true," he was saying.

There was a long silence. And then unbelievably, there came the calm voice of an older woman. "Yes, yes, of course. I can understand your concern," she murmured. "But have no fear. My granddaughter is sleeping upstairs. We mustn't bother her."

My eyes practically bugged out of my head and I stared at Penelope. She was staring back at me, her mouth open.

"Yes, indeed, this darling girl is my granddaughter," the voice continued. "I thank you so very much for bringing her home this morning, she gets into the most terrible mischief!"

Penelope was still staring at me. "I - I don't understand," she stammered.

I shrugged. "I don't either."

"Is she really your grandmother?" Her eyes widened, and she took a step back from me. "A-a-re you a witch?"

I chuckled softly. "No," I said firmly. "I am most certainly not a witch!" I stood up and brushed myself off, waiting until I heard the door open and close and the sound of horses trotting away from the house. Then I motioned to Penelope. "Come with me," I said.

I strode up to the front door, squared my shoulders and knocked loudly. Penelope was standing behind me, looking for once like she had no idea what to do with herself. Her hands kept fluttering from her apron pockets to her bonnet and back again, and she coughed nervously.

A moment later the door swung open and an elderly woman peered out, looking suspiciously from side to side. She was tall and thin, and she was wearing the same dark dress, apron and bonnet that Penelope and her mother wore. Her eyes locked with mine, and she stared at me so intently, I felt like she could read my mind. Finally, after studying us for several seconds, she waved us inside, slamming the door behind us.

We followed her into the living room, which was a bare and empty space with just a few chairs in it. And in the corner, biting her nails and looking like she was going to pass out, sat a very pale and very small looking Sheila.

"You are not my granddaughters." The woman said it simply, sitting down and crossing her legs. Her eyes kept wandering back to my jeans.

"Yes, ma'am," I said, sliding into one of the remaining chairs. Penelope stayed standing near the doorway, clutching her bonnet in her white-knuckled hands. "I apologize. We, um..."

"Never mind!" The woman waved her hand in the air. "It doesn't matter. I must admit, I was very taken aback when Mr. and Mrs. Padgett brought you here. I may not know a lot about myself, but one thing I do know - I am no grandmother! But you seem like good kids, and if you are hiding from something, who am I to blow your cover?"

"Blow their cover?" Penelope broke in suddenly. "What does that mean?"

I stole a glance at Sheila. I'm no expert on languages, but I'm pretty sure people didn't use that expression in 1739. Sheila didn't seem to notice, though. She was still staring ahead and biting her nails.

The woman seemed flustered. "Er, I mean - I did not want to reveal your deception. However, it is best that you move on now. I shall bring you some tea and then you should be on your way." She stood up and walked out of the room, leaving Sheila, Penelope and me alone.

I stood up and rushed over to Sheila, leaning over to give her a big hug. "I have the medallion," I whispered in her ear. "Come on, it's time."

She stood up, and we both faced Penelope. "You're not going to understand this, but we need to leave now." I reached over and kissed her on her cheek. "You have been very kind to us, and we wish you all the best."

Penelope smiled at us. "I shall miss you," she said.

"We'll miss you too," Sheila replied. "And by the way, definitely keep on learning to read. Where we come from, girls can do everything boys can do, and you should stick up for yourself!"

With that, I took the medallion out of my pocket, grabbed Sheila's hand, and cried, "March 14, 2011! March 14, 2011! March 14, 2011!"

******

♥ March 15, 2011 ♥

Dear Diary,

So that's the whole crazy story. I can't believe I wrote it all down yesterday! My hand is killing me. It's practically falling off from writing so much.

We landed right back in the clubhouse, and it was like we had never left - It was still Monday afternoon, and even our leftover snack was still there! Thankfully, it seemed that nobody had even noticed we were gone.

The only problem was that Sheila was still wearing the apron and dress we had gotten from Penelope. And her regular clothes must have gotten lost in the race to Mrs. Hodgson's house. We couldn't find them anywhere.

I gave Sheila some normal clothes, but before she had time to change, SRJ burst into the room, took one look at her and started shrieking. "It's not fair!" he yelled. "I want a costume too!"

Luckily, I was able to distract him with an old Superman costume from the playroom. Sheila chuckled as she pulled on a pair of my jeans. "Things sure haven't changed around here," she said.

I rolled my eyes. "That's for sure." As I stuffed Penelope's old dress onto a shelf in the back of my closet, I felt something in the apron pocket, and pulled out the old newspaper Sheila had taken from Penelope's room. I unfolded it and shuddered as I looked at the date: July 5th, 1739.

The mind boggles.

******

At school today the minutes ticked by so slowly, I thought I would scream. But in history class, something happened that caught my attention.

We were sitting in third period, reading from our textbooks, and my eyes kept closing in spite of themselves. I was e-x-h-a-u-s-t-e-d! I had just started dozing off, when Mrs. Santini said, "Ok, class, turn the page. Who can read to us about Penelope Barker and the Edenton Tea Party?"

My ears perked up. Penelope? Edenton?

"Sheila, would you do the honors?"

Sheila straightened up in her chair and started randomly flipping through the pages of her book. She had that deer-in-headlights look kids get when they've been caught daydreaming. Finally she gave

Mrs. Santini a sheepish smile. "Um, what page were we on again?" A titter went through the room, and out of the corner of my eye, I could see MTS and Jessica giggling.

"Page 345, Sheila." Mrs. Santini shook her head.

Sheila cleared her throat and began reading: "Penelope Barker was born on June 17, 1728 in Edenton, North Carolina. Born Penelope Padgett, her parents were Samuel Padgett, a physician and planter, and Elizabeth Blount, the daughter of an important politician. Remembered as a dutiful and well-behaved child, Penelope had two sisters, Elizabeth and Margaret."

I sat bolt upright in my chair and did a quick calculation in my head. 1728??? That would mean the Penelope Padgett in our textbook would have been... eleven in 1739. I swallowed hard, excitement rising in my chest, and turned to face Sheila, willing her to look up at me. But she just kept on reading, her voice betraying a light tremor.

"Unfortunately, Penelope Padgett suffered through many tragic events when she was just a teenager. Her father and her sister Elizabeth both d-died, and Penelope took responsibility for Elizabeth's children, Isabella, Robert and John. Several years later, she married her sister's widower, John Hodgson, and had two more sons of her own, Samuel and Thomas. Her husband died just a year after marrying her, leaving her to care for five children all on her own. She later remarried two more times."

Wow. It sounded like Penelope had had a really hard life! But wait a minute... I raised my hand.

"Um, Mrs. Santini?"

"Yes, Janie," Mrs. Santini said, looking up from her textbook and frowning in my direction. "What is it?"

"Well, it's just – There's a mistake in the book." I drummed my fingers nervously on my desk. I'm not one of the those kids that raises their hand all the time in class, and to be honest, talking in front of everybody makes me a bit nervous. I don't know why, but it does.

"A mistake?" Mrs. Santini was still frowning.

I glanced over at Sheila, and she grinned at me.

"Well, it's just that – Penelope's sisters' names were Elizabeth and Sarah. Not Margaret."

Mrs. Santini just kind of stood there for a few seconds. Then she said, "How could you possibly know a thing like that?"

"I, um, read a book about her once."

"Well, Janie, this is a very good textbook, and it doesn't usually make mistakes. You're probably misremembering." Mrs. Santini smiled kindly.

My face grew hot. "Um, actually, I'm pretty sure I'm not."

Mrs. Santini blinked several times, looking nonplussed. Finally she said, "Well, Janie, since you seem so certain, why don't you Google it for us now at the class computer station?" She had her hand on her hip, and she was watching me expectantly.

Oh no. I got up slowly, trying to ignore the sinking feeling in my stomach, and made my way over to the computer station. Suddenly I wasn't so sure of myself. What if the history books got it wrong, or she had another sister? Mrs. Santini turned on the projector while I double clicked on the internet browser and carefully typed in the name "Penelope Barker". I don't think I ever remember the class so quiet – I swear, you could hear a pin drop!

I opened the Wikipedia entry and quickly scanned the page, dismayed to discover that it didn't mention any sisters. I closed it and went on to the next search result, a lump rising in my throat. And then, before I even started reading, Ben White pointed excitedly at the whiteboard.

"Mrs. Santini, I see it! Janie's right!"

Sure enough, there it was: Elizabeth and Sarah. I breathed a sigh of relief leaned back in my chair, a triumphant smile on my face.

Mrs. Santini regarded me with surprise. "Well, Janie, I had no idea we had an expert on Penelope Barker in our class! I guess we'll have to write to the textbook company and point out their error!"

I nodded, and as I headed back to my seat, I couldn't help adding under my breath, "Yeah, and she wasn't all that dutiful and well-behaved, either."

Mrs. Santini nodded to Sheila to keep on reading, and she cleared her throat and picked up the book.

"In October 1774, several months after the famous Boston Tea Party, in which American colonists destroyed tea cargo to protest the taxes they had to pay to the British king, Barker organized a women's protest of her own. She wrote a statement calling for people to stop using British goods, and got 51 local women to sign it. A famous female activist in the period leading up to the American Revolution, Barker was reported to have said, 'Maybe it has only been men who have protested the king up to now. That only means we women have taken too long to let our voices be heard. We are signing our names to a document, not hiding ourselves behind costumes like the men in Boston did at their tea party. The British will know who we are. Patience and Modesty have been my inspiration.'"

Sheila stopped reading, her mouth open, and met my eyes. I grinned at her. Patience and Modesty, indeed. Now *that* sounded like the Penelope I knew. And clearly, she had learned how to read.

******

♥ March 17, 2011 ♥

Dear Diary,

Yesterday Sheila couldn't come over after school, so we had to wait until this afternoon to meet up in the clubhouse and talk about everything that's been going on.

"We should go on another adventure!" Sheila said, plopping down on the floor.

"Hold your horses," I said. "We just barely made it back from the last one!"

Sheila giggled. "I mean a different kind of adventure. Something a bit less - dramatic." She held her hand out. "Can I see the medallion?"

I blinked. "Uh, I guess so," I said, reaching into my pocket and pulling it out. "But no funny business, ok?"

"No funny business." Sheila agreed, a tiny smile playing on her lips. She took the medallion and turned it around in her hands. And then, before I could stop her, she grabbed my arm. "June 21st, 1985! June 21st, 1985! June 21st, 1985!"

******

This time we landed in a green, grassy meadow in the middle of nowhere.

Sheila stood up and straightened her shirt, holding out her hand to help me up. I turned away from her, clenching my fists in anger. "I can't believe you did that," I muttered under my breath. "Sometimes you are such a total -"

"Oh, come on," she said, "Don't worry so much! This'll be fun!" She looked around and pointed to a bus stop about 300 yards away. In the distance, I could hear a truck speeding by. "Let's go see if there's a sign over there or anything," she said. "Oh come on, Janie, I promise that the first second anything looks wrong, we'll leave right away. Don't be such a spoil sport!"

She held up the medallion, allowing the light to reflect off its shiny surface. It shone brightly in the sun. Then she handed it to me. "Here. I'm sorry, I shouldn't have done that."

"You can say that again," I said, shaking my head. I put the medallion in my pocket and stood up grumpily, feeling queasy. "I guess we could explore a little. But then we're going right home!" Sheila was acting like a little kid!

We trudged towards the bus stop in an uneasy silence, and I unzipped my sweatshirt, taking it off and tying it absentmindedly around my waist. At least here I wouldn't have to wear any old dresses with *bonnets.*

"Wow, look at that!" Sheila said, pointing excitedly at the bus stop. "They have an ad for that old movie we saw on Netflix with your parents last week!"

I stared at the placard. *Back to the Future – Coming Soon to a Theater Near You.*

"Didn't your mom say that that movie came out when she was eleven?" Sheila was saying. "I wonder what she was like at our age..." Her voice trailed off. Then her eyes grew wide. "Wait a minute! She grew up in your house, didn't she?"

"Oh no you don't!" I said firmly. "Don't even think about that. It would be *way* too creepy. Plus, we don't have any idea where we are." *I don't want to see what my house looked like when my mother was little, anyway,* I thought. *Her room was probably spotless.* "I think we should just go home now."

I stopped abruptly and grabbed Sheila's arm, motioning her to be quiet, as a group of five girls approached the bus stop. They looked young – maybe eight or nine years old – and they were talking excitedly. Luckily, they were too wrapped up in their conversation to notice us.

"I'm getting a Walkman for my birthday!" one of them was saying proudly. She had big, puffy blonde hair and a tiny button nose, and was wearing a jeans jacket and bright, pink leg warmers. *Leg warmers in the summer?* I found myself wondering. Sometimes I have the most random thoughts.

"That's awesome!" a second girl said. She was shorter, with brown hair and glasses, and she looked oddly familiar. "My big sister has one, and I'm totally jealous! She screams at me every time I go near it. I totally hope I get one for my birthday next year." *How many times could someone use the word "totally" in one sentence?*

"What are you doing for your birthday party?" a third girl with big bangs asked.

"Oh, I'm just going to have a few kids over for a movie night. We're gonna watch a movie on the VCR! Don't worry, you guys are all invited."

The girls grew quiet as three older kids, holding enormous Slurpees in old-fashioned cups, came and sat down on the bench next to them. "Move your stuff over!" one of them said rudely, pushing the girls' bags onto the ground. "Do you think you guys own this bus stop?"

"Hey!" the short, familiar girl said, picking up her bag from the floor. "What's wrong with you guys? You could have just asked."

"*What's wrong with you guys!*" the older kid mimicked. His friends laughed.

Seriously? These kids were at least two or three years older than the girls. They looked our age. Were they really trying to pick a fight with them? *Who does that?* Sheila and I exchanged worried glances, and I had a sudden memory of the time RJ was pushed off a swing by a bigger kid and needed three stitches in his eyebrow.

"Hey, pick on someone your own size!" I was startled to hear the sound of my own voice. *Had I just said that?* The older kids stared at me, not saying anything, and Sheila looked as if she was going to faint. The short girl just stood there, gaping at me with her mouth open.

The minutes dragged on in silence, until a bus finally pulled into the stop and the older kids got on. The girls were noticeably relieved.

"Hey, you look a lot like my sister," the short girl said, smiling at me as she followed her friends onto a second bus that had pulled up behind the first. "I don't know if she would have stuck up for me like that, though."

Why did she look so familiar?

I was getting that queasy feeling again, and I suddenly realized that I had to get out of there, pronto. Without another word, I reached into my pocket and grabbed the medallion, placing my hand on Sheila's shoulder. "March 14, 2011!"

******

Again we screamed, as we felt ourselves falling.

Thump. We landed hard and looked around, surprised and relieved to find ourselves sprawled out on the floor of the clubhouse.

"Holy Smokes!" Sheila said, picking herself up off the ground and staring at the medallion with wonder.

I stayed where I was on the floor, too shocked to say anything. No matter how many times we did that, I didn't think I'd ever get used to it.

"Do you realize what this means, Janie?" Sheila said, looking from the medallion to me and back again. She jumped up and down and squealed with excitement. "This is going to be *so much fun!* We can travel through time, go wherever we want, and when we want to come home, all we have to do is say so!" She did a little dance.

I coughed and blinked, trying to focus and wondering vaguely why the room looked as if it had just had a new coat of paint.

"Sheila?" I could hear what sounded like my mother's voice calling from inside the house. "Sheila, I need your help, sweetie! Come on out of the clubhouse now, ok?"

"We're coming," I answered, looking at Sheila with a puzzled expression. I opened the door and walked outside. *Why was my mother calling Sheila?*

"Sheila!" It was my mother's voice again, but when I saw her, I realized that something was terribly wrong. She may have been calling Sheila, but she was looking straight at me.

TO BE CONTINUED...

The Day My Mom Got Grounded!

♥ March 20, 2011 ♥

Dear Diary,

I don't really have that much time to write today, and I still haven't finished telling you the story! So before SRJ comes in to bother me, I'll try to get down as much as I can...

******

So there we were, standing outside the clubhouse, and my mom was asking me to clean my room - but for some reason, she kept calling me Sheila!

Before I could reply, my mom turned around and hurried back toward the house. "Your father is having an important client over for dinner tonight," she called out over her shoulder, as she opened the screen door. "I need you to clean your room and help me straighten the living room, ok?"

I managed a nod and looked over at Sheila, who was standing right behind me with her mouth open. We stared at each other.

"Your mom looks kind of weird, doesn't she," Sheila finally said. "Did she color her hair?"

"Her hair?" I replied, annoyed. "Her *hair*? How can you think about her *hair* at a time like this?"

"Sorry," Sheila grinned sheepishly. "I just meant, she doesn't look like herself. And why did she call you Sheila?"

"I don't know, maybe she just mixed up our names." I picked up the medallion and dropped it into my pocket. "She always calls me Karen and she sometimes even calls my Dad RJ. Anyway, come on – let's go to my room so we can talk while I clean it up. We have a lot to talk about!"

"We sure do," Sheila agreed.

******

We walked inside and I gasped, looking around. Where was our piano? And why were the living room walls *peach*? Sheila tapped me on the shoulder, a worried look on her face. "This doesn't look right".

"No," I murmured. "It doesn't. And it doesn't *smell* right either." It smelled like strawberries, like – *Grandma Sollie*. For no reason, I had a sudden image of the cheese and tomato sandwiches with the crusts cut off that Grandma always made when I came over to her house after kindergarten, when I was little. And of the way my mom cried when she came back from the hospital when I was nine and told me that Grandma had died. A wistful knot formed in my stomach.

I walked over to the bookshelf in the far corner of the room – the old bookshelf, then chipped and sagging, that my parents had ultimately decided to throw out when we moved in. I remembered that bookshelf. Except now it was brand new...

"Sheila, what on Earth are you doing?" I was startled out of my thoughts by the sound of my mother's voice. "And what are you wearing? Go upstairs right now, change your clothes, and clean up that mess of yours. Honestly!"

She called me Sheila again.

I looked into my mother's eyes, and suddenly it all became shockingly, horrifyingly clear. *This wasn't my mother. It was Grandma Sollie!* Somehow, instead of going home, we had ended up in my grandparents' house, and we were still in the past!

******

I stared at Grandma Sollie, too stunned to say anything. She was younger, and she looked a lot like my mom – but now that I was really looking, I could see it was definitely her. Tears welled up in my eyes as I resisted an overwhelming urge to throw myself into her arms and hug her. I couldn't do that, at least not yet.

"Uh... O.K. uh...Mom," I cleared my throat, turning around and beckoning to Sheila. "I'm going upstairs now and I'll, uh, clean up my room right away."

I walked towards the stairs, grabbing Sheila by the arm and pulling her behind me. "We *have* to talk," I whispered loudly. "Come on!"

The stairs looked just like they did in my house, except that they were covered in soft, blue carpeting. Old-fashioned looking pictures hung on the wall. The one of my mom and Auntie Karen eating ice-cream cones outside on the front steps, which hung over the piano in our house. One I hadn't seen before of Grandpa Charlie when he was younger, holding up some kind of a trophy. One of Grandma Sollie, holding Grandpa Charlie's hand and looking incredibly happy.

And one of a girl about eleven years old, holding a dog on a leash and grinning. And I'll be a monkey's uncle if she didn't look incredibly, exactly, astoundingly *just like me.*

I paused in front of the picture of Auntie Karen, taking in her brown hair and glasses and shuddering as I remembered the girl at the bus stop.

"What in the world is going on here?" Sheila stage-whispered, as we reached the top of the stairs.

"Shhh!" I hissed. "Just wait a second." I yanked Sheila in the direction of what I hoped and guessed would be my mother's room. The door was closed and it had a big sign on it with a picture of a stop sign and the words DO NOT ENTER!! scrawled across it in bold, red crayon. I ignored the sign and pulled the door open, gasping yet again as I looked inside.

My mother's room was a mess.

******

"Somehow we've ended up in my grandparents' house!" I started to explain as I flopped down on my mother's bed, pushing a pile of (dirty?) laundry onto the floor.

As I spoke, I glanced around the room nervously. A bunch of posters hung on the wall – The Beatles, Madonna, and a few others I didn't recognize – and a huge box of old cassette tapes lay open on the floor. I had never listened to a tape before. My parents had a whole collection, which I looked through one day

74

when I was bored, but my mom's old tape player didn't work. A collection of stuffed animals and funny looking dolls was strewn across the carpet, near the closet. A pink girl's desk stood in the corner, buried under piles of paper and books.

"Your grandparents?" Sheila looked blank for a moment as it sunk in. "Oh! So that's why she called you Sheila! She thought you were your... Wow." She leaned back on the bedpost, which was also pink, and swung her feet onto the bed.

"Don't put your shoes on the bed," I said automatically, tapping her feet.

"Seriously? Have you seen this place?" She gestured to the desk, and then to the closet which was literally overflowing with piles of clothes. "I really don't think shoes on the bed are an issue."

"I guess you're right. I can't believe it though..." *Who would have thought my mom would be such a slob?*

Suddenly Sheila reached over and grabbed a small spiral notebook that was sitting on my mom's night table. It was also pink and had the words "My Diary – Top Secret!" written across the front in magic marker. Sheila turned it over in her hands, inspecting it. Then she looked up at me, raised an eyebrow and grinned.

"No!" I said instinctively, reaching out to grab the diary. "We are *not* reading my mom's secret diary! Imagine if she did that to me! I'd never forgive her."

Sheila moved her hand away, holding the diary above her head. "But this is different," she insisted. "Would you mind if time travelers from the future read *your* diary?" She smiled mischievously and awaited my reply.

I couldn't resist a smile. "I guess when you put it that way..." When would I ever have another opportunity to find out about my mom's innermost thoughts, and what she was like when she was my age? "Come to think of it, she has said a few times she wished she had saved her diaries for me. Grandma Sollie threw them out when my mom went to college."

"See! She wants you to read it! And anyway, we have a mystery on our hands. If we're gonna get out of here, we need all the information we can get!" Without waiting for me to answer, she opened the diary and started reading aloud.

I moved uncomfortably on the bed, an uncertain feeling in my gut. Reading someone else's diary was never right, and yet –

******

Dear Diary,

Ok, this is the last straw! Last night I came home from ballet and found Karen in my room, playing with my Barbie Dream House. I told her she could play with it sometimes, but only when I was home! She ran out when she saw me coming, but I could tell she moved the Barbie furniture around and ruined my setup. I made a new DO NOT ENTER sign, and if that doesn't work, I'll have to think of something else.

Marcy was supposed to come over today and bake cookies with me, but at the last minute she told me she had decided to go over to Jen's house. ☹ I think we're still best friends, but lately she always seems to want to be with Jen. She says it's just easier to go over to Jen's because she lives closer. Sometimes it seems like me and Jen are fighting over Marcy, and it's soooooo unfair. Why can't I ever be the one they're fighting over?

******

Sheila stopped reading and looked up at me. "Wow. Your mom sounds like a real kid!"

"What do you mean, dorkbrain? She is a real kid! What do you think, that she was born a grownup?"

Sheila rolled her eyes and flipped a few pages back. She continued to read.

******

◊ March 13, 1985 ◊

Dear Diary,

Dad's been acting really weird lately. Yesterday, I went into his study when he wasn't home to find my Sweet Valley High book. There was no one there, so I sat down to read on the couch. And then, suddenly when I looked up, he was standing there, totally out of breath. It was s-t-r-a-n-g-e! When he saw me, he went totally white and started muttering something about running up the stairs. Which was weird, because his study's on the first floor.

Then this morning, he told me that he needed to talk to me about something after school. He looked very serious, like when I got a C- on my math test last month. Except he wasn't angry. I have to —

******

Sheila stopped midsentence and snapped the book shut, as the door swung open. I looked up, startled.

"Sheila! You haven't even started cleaning your room!" Grandma Sollie had the same expression on her face that my mom did, when she was really exasperated. "Well, there's no time for that now." She looked at her watch and back at me. "You have to be at ballet practice in fifteen minutes. Get your stuff together, we'll be leaving in five. And don't forget to brush your hair."

She turned sharply and left the room, closing the door behind her. I looked around, frantically searching for my mom's ballet stuff. My mom was forever trying to convince me to take ballet lessons, but I never wanted to. Too prissy.

I spotted a small, pink backpack slung across the desk chair. As I ruffled inside, I saw with relief that it contained a white leotard and a pink tutu. I made a face at Sheila. "She sure does like pink."

"Yeah," Sheila answered, wrinkling her nose. "I'm glad *I'm* not gonna have to wear that."

"That's going to be the least of my troubles," I said. "You may not remember this, but I don't actually *know* any ballet. How am I going to get through a whole class? And anyway – where *is* she?!"

"I don't know…" Sheila said, "And what if she's there?"

"I guess we're just going to have to go and find out."

******

"Ok, we're ready!" I called out to Grandma Sollie, as we came down the stairs.

"Shei— I mean, Susan's parents are coming home late today, so she'd like to come with me to ballet. S-s-Susan's new at school."

Grandma Sollie smiled at Sheila and shrugged her shoulders. "Nice to meet you, honey. I don't see any problem with that. As long as it's ok with your parents."

"Oh, it is." Sheila grinned at me.

We climbed into the back seat of the old-fashioned, blue Honda parked in front of the house and put on our seatbelts.

"I'm glad to see you're buckling up, girls, but I'm not sure it's necessary in the back seat." We glanced at each other. *Weird.*

As we slowly made our way across town, I looked out the window with my mouth open. We passed the 7-11 on Montrose Road that had been there as long as I could remember – and it looked almost exactly the same, just newer somehow. The Barnes and Noble that had been next door was gone, replaced by something called Crowne Books. Or rather – Crowne books was to be replaced by Barnes and Noble, sometime in the future.

Then we passed a big, empty lot on the right, and Sheila nudged me. "Montgomery Mall is gone!" she whispered.

"You mean it hasn't been built yet," I whispered back. We giggled.

At last we pulled up in front what used to be – or rather, what would become -- The Bagel Place. Except it was painted orange and had a big green sign on it that read, "Molly's Ballet".

"Ok, girls," Grandma Sollie called as we got out of the car. "Your father will be here to pick you up at five-thirty sharp. Don't hold him up. He has an important dinner tonight".

******

Inside, everybody seemed to know where to go. We stood uncertainly by the door, trying not to look too confused, when a girl with straight black hair, braces and a huge smile bounded up to us.

"Oh my God, Sheila! You are *not* going to believe what Kevin said to me this morning. Where *were* you? I thought you were sick or something." Without waiting for a reply she grabbed my hand and pulled me toward the locker room. "Come on, let's go get dressed."

When she saw Sheila following us, the girl turned to her and demanded, "Who are you?"

"This is my cousin Susan," I managed. "She's visiting from Detroit."

"Nice to meet you, Susan." The girl stuck out her hand and shook Sheila's hand matter of factly. Then she turned to me. "You never told me you had a cousin your age that lived in Detroit!" she added accusingly. "So, you want to watch the class?" She rolled her eyes. "It's pretty boring. Sheila and I have wanted to quit for ages, but our parents won't let us."

Now *this* was getting interesting. My mom was always telling me how much she loved ballet when she was my age. I grinned to myself. My mom was cool. I tried to remember if she had ever mentioned a friend who took ballet lessons with her, but my mind came up blank.

"I'll just listen to my ipod, or whatev – Ow!!" Sheila shot me a questioning look, as I elbowed her sharply in the ribs.

"Uh..." I croaked, then cleared my throat. "Shei – I mean – Susan has been thinking of taking ballet lessons."

The girl looked at me, then at Sheila, and then back at me again. "Ok, whatever. Come on, let's go get dressed."

******

"Sheila, what's wrong with you today?" Molly, the ballet teacher, stood next to me and frowned. "It's almost as if you don't remember any of the steps! Here, let me show you." She held my waist and pointed with her foot. "See, it's like this. One, two, three. One two three."

I cast a worried glance at Sheila. It was hopeless. I couldn't dance if my life depended on it.

"Marcy, what's wrong with Sheila today?" a girl with long, blond curls called out from the other side of the studio. The girls standing next to her snickered. "It's like she has *three* left feet, instead of her usual two."

"Shut up, Jen," Marcy looked at me, uncomfortable. "I don't know why Jen has to be so mean. I wish you guys could become friends."

So this was my mom's best friend Marcy. And Jen - the girl from the diary who was trying to steal Marcy away!

"Well, she's right." I brushed the hair away from my eyes and put on my best brave grin. "I haven't been practicing lately, and I'm not myself today."

"I'll say," Marcy said, doing a pirouette, her straight, black hair whirling behind her. "If I didn't know any better, I'd say you'd been kidnapped by aliens and replaced by a clone."

Sheila coughed and looked at me, raising her eyebrow. "Yeah, Marcy. Sheila really hasn't been herself lately."

******

Back in the locker room, Marcy was very quiet as she changed back into her jeans and tee-shirt. I could feel her staring at me, but every time I turned around, she immediately looked away. Finally she spoke.

"Did you tell your parents about the A you got on our math test last week?"

"Uh, yeah." I answered, pulling on my socks. "My dad was really happy. I don't think I've ever – "

"We didn't *have* a math test last week." Marcy faced me squarely, arms folded across her chest. "And you've never gotten an A in math in your life. What the heck is going on here, Sheila? Or whoever you are!"

I sank onto the bench, putting my sneaker down and trying desperately to decide what to tell her. If I told her the truth, would she even believe me? And what if she blabbed about it to other people? On the other hand, maybe if she knew what was going on, she could help us get home.

"Ok." I picked up my sneaker and started putting it on again. "I'll tell you, but you have to promise not to tell anyone. And I'm warning you – you're probably not going to believe me."

******

The three of us walked outside, nobody saying anything. Marcy kept looking from me to Sheila, shaking her head wordlessly. Then she cleared her throat.

"So, um, maybe you guys should come over to my house, so we can talk."

Sheila nodded her head. "That sounds like a good idea," she said before I had a chance to answer. Just then, the old blue Honda pulled up at the curb. The man inside leaned over and rolled down the window.

Grandpa Charlie!

My mouth dropped open as I stared at him. He looked almost exactly as I remembered him from all the pictures we had at home, except much younger. He was wearing a button-down, striped shirt with a tie, and brown pants and sneakers. And a huge smile creased his face.

"Sheila!" he exclaimed. He was positively beaming. "You have no idea how happy I am to see you! I was worried sick!" His face grew sterner, and he gestured to Sheila. "When your friend goes home, we're going to have to have a little talk. You have what you took from me, right?"

Sheila and I exchanged worried glances. *What I took?*

"Uh.." I barely managed a croak. "Sure. I think so. But Dad," I swallowed hard. "Marcy invited us over for dinner. Would that be ok? We can talk later, when I get home."

Grandpa Charlie sighed. "Sheila, I really wish you'd tell me these things before I drag out to pick you up – especially on a day like today. I guess it's ok, though. Call me when you're ready to come home."

******

"So basically, yeah, we're time-travelers from the future, and I'm Sheila's daughter." I stuck out my hand. "My name's Janie. Nice to meet you. And her real name is Sheila."

We were sitting in Marcy's room, on the thick, purple carpet that covered her floor. Thank goodness it wasn't pink. I had explained the entire situation to her, even pulling out the medallion to show her the inscription. She had listened carefully, interrupting only to ask the occasional question.

She reached out and shook my hand, her eyes wide. "Jeez. I ... I don't really know what to say. I'm not even sure I believe you."

"Well..." I pointed to Sheila's orange Crocs. "Have you ever seen shoes like this before?"

Marcy laughed. "I'd been wondering about those. No offence, but they're kind of ugly."

Sheila smiled. "Yeah. For some reason they're wildly popular in the future, though."

"But that isn't actual proof." Marcy continued. "How do I know you didn't just make those yourselves, or buy them in some kind of funky store?"

"Yeah..." I stared thoughtfully at the River Phoenix poster that hung on the wall next to her dresser. My mom had shown me the movie *Stand by Me* on Netflix, so I knew who River Phoenix was. She had told me he was one of her favorite actors when she was a kid. Then suddenly it hit me.

"Wait a minute – what's the date today?"

"June 22nd, why?" Marcy answered.

"Oh. My. God." I jumped up and started pacing around the room nervously. "Because I just realized, tomorrow – June 23rd – there is going to be a horrible plane crash! My mom's second cousin Emma, who lived in Ireland, was on that plane! My mom didn't know her very well, but we attend a memorial service for her every year, on June 23rd."

Sheila looked startled. "Your mom's cousin is supposed to be in a plane crash tomorrow?"

I sat back down, shaking, as the implications of what I was saying sank in. "We have to do something! Warn her not to get on the plane – or better yet, figure out how to delay or prevent the plane from taking off!"

Marcy was staring at me, her face frozen in a look of surprised panic.

"Please, Marcy," I pleaded with her. "You've got to believe us. I look just like my mom, right? And we're dressed funny, and when we have time, we'll tell you all about the internet, ipods, cell phones, and what happens in *Back to the Future*, which is coming out in a couple of weeks. I know it's a lot to ask, but I promise you, we'll be able to prove it to you eventually."

As I spoke, Sheila reached into her back pocket and pulled out her ipod. "I'm such a dummy, I can't believe I forgot about this." She turned it on and handed it to Marcy. "Here, listen to this."

Marcy's eyes widened even more, if that was even possible, as she put on the earphones and listened. "It's like a tiny Discman!" she finally sputtered. "And the sound is incredible!" She stood up and beckoned to us impatiently, suddenly all business. "All right guys, what we need now is a plan. First to save your cousin. And then to find your mom and get you guys back home."

******

♥ March 20, 2011 ♥

Dear Diary,

Yes, it's still today, Sunday. I haven't written this much in a million years! Then again, I guess this is the first time that something really interesting has happened to me. Not that my life isn't interesting, but you know what I mean. I had to take a break earlier, because SRJ came running into my room crying like a hysterical baby. When I asked him what was wrong, he just climbed up on my bed and sat there, sucking his thumb and clinging to his old baby blanket. After a few minutes, my mom came up after him, opening the door and sighing. It turned out all that crying was just because he couldn't have another chocolate-chip cookie. As if three cookies weren't enough! I'm telling you, that kid is spoiled. I *never* got more than two cookies when I was his age, and I didn't go around crying about it! My mom scooped him off the bed and carried him back downstairs, winking at me and apologizing for bursting into my room without knocking.

Things with my mom have been kind of different since I got back. But I'll tell you about that later.

Anyway, right after that I got a phone call, and you'll never guess who it was. CALVIN! He was calling me to get the English homework. He never knows what the homework is, and his backpack is always a mess. It's lucky he called me and not Sheila, though. If he had called her, she probably would have had a heart attack or something. And I'd never hear the end of it.

Speaking of Sheila, my hand is about to fall off, but I *have* to get to the end of the story. So we were in Marcy's room, remember? Trying to figure out how to save my cousin and find my mom ...

***** ✱✱✱✱✱✱

"Marcy, Sheila's dad is here to pick her up!"

Marcy looked at me, panicked. "What should we do?" she whispered. "We still have to make a plan. And you definitely shouldn't go back to your grandparents' house. It took me *half an hour* to figure out you aren't Sheila. You'll be lucky if it takes them ten minutes!"

Sheila and I glanced at each other nervously.

"Marcy!" Marcy's mom called up the stairs again, her voice impatient. "Did you hear me? I said Sheila's dad is here to pick her up!"

Just then the door opened, and Grandpa Charlie walked in. He was wearing jeans and a red, plaid flannel shirt, and he had a faint, familiar smell. *Old Spice.* I closed my eyes and breathed in, suddenly struck by a vague memory of sitting in his lap on the swing in our backyard when I was really little, listening to him read *Blueberries for Sal.*

The sound of his voice jolted me back to reality. "Hi Marcy," he said, frowning at Sheila as she grabbed her ipod and stuffed it quickly into her back pocket. He turned to me. "Sheila, come on. We really have to get going. We have a lot to talk about!"

I just sat there, looking at Marcy, and then at Grandpa Charlie.

"Um," Marcy stood up and pulled at the leg of her jeans, scratching her ankle. "Actually, I was wondering if Ja – I mean, Sheila and Susan could sleep over tonight. We still have a lot of math homework to finish."

"I'm sorry, honey, she can't," Grandpa Charlie said, placing a firm hand on my shoulder. "We have to go home now." He leaned over and added quietly, "We need to talk about the medallion."

I gasped and jumped up as if stung by a bee. *He knew about the medallion.*

"H-h-h-h" I stuttered, then tried again. "How do you know about the medallion?"

The room was so quiet you could hear a pin drop. Grandpa Charlie looked at me quizzically, furrowing his brow and biting his thumbnail. When he spoke again, his voice was low.

"You're not Sheila." It was a statement rather than a question. His eyes darted from me to Sheila and then to Marcy. "Who are you?" he finally asked. "And where's Sheila?"

"Um." A sense of panic welled up inside me. "I-i-i don't know. I mean, I know who I am, of course. I, um, just don't know where Sheila is," I finished lamely.

"Janie found the medallion when she was seven, on a family vacation to Miami," Sheila broke in. I smiled at her gratefully as she continued. "It had her name on it and everything! I mean, it's not like we took it from anyone. The inscription on it was written in a secret language we made up together for our clubhouse, *four years* after she found it! It said, 'Janie, hold the medallion and say the date you want to visit three times' or something like that. Well, we did what it said, and we ended up in an open field, but then when we tried to go home, it brought us here! And before that, we took a trip back to 1739!"

Again there was silence, and even though I was looking at Sheila, I could feel Grandpa Charlie's eyes boring into me.

"Janie." He said my name simply. I looked over at him and was shocked to see tears in his eyes. "I knew this could happen one day, but I never thought -" His voice caught, and I realized he was trying not to cry. "You're Sheila's girl. Of course! How could I have missed that? Come here sweetie."

He opened his arms, and as I leaned in and put my head on his shoulder, I knew everything was going to be ok.

******

"All right, girls," Grandpa Charlie sat down on Marcy's bed, moving aside a pile of *Seventeen* magazines. "I guess I'll just have to start at the beginning."

"Wait -" Marcy said. "My mom's expecting us to come down to dinner now. Does Sheila's mom know about the medallion too? And what about Karen?"

"No, Marcy, they don't." Grandpa Charlie stood back up. "Come to think of it, it might be a good idea for Sheila and Susan -" he paused, grinning sheepishly, "I mean, Janie and Sheila - to stay here tonight after all. We don't need to stir up any more trouble than we already have."

"I'm sure it'll be fine with my mom," Marcy said. "Why don't you guys go for a walk and talk things over. You can come back here after dinner, and we can make a plan." Marcy seemed to be a very sensible person. I could see why my mom liked her. She didn't freak out when things got weird, and she always seemed to know what to do. Come to think of it, she kind of reminded me of Sheila.

"Great plan." Grandpa Charlie reached over and tweaked Marcy's ear. Then he glanced at his watch, a ginormous one that seemed to double as a miniature calculator. "We'll be back in an hour."

******

I shivered as we walked down Marcy's street, making our way around old-fashioned parked cars, bicycles and the occasional motorcycle. It was cool for the end of June. Grandpa Charlie handed me his sweater, and I shrugged it on, pulling it tightly around me.

"The medallion has been in our family for generations," Grandpa Charlie began. "According to family legend, it originated in ancient Egypt, at the time of Ramses the Great. And it's been passed down ever since, from grandparent to grandchild, always skipping a generation."

"Why?" Sheila asked. "I mean, why doesn't it go from parent to child?"

"That's a good question, Sheila. Nobody really knows. The origins of the medallion remain shrouded in mystery. My guess is that it's meant to allow the family to maintain a semblance of normalcy. Each Bearer of the Medallion is born into a perfectly ordinary family, and it's only when they come of age that the medallion is passed on to them by their grandmother or grandfather."

"I wonder..." Sheila started saying.

"What?" my grandfather asked. "Please don't hesitate to ask."

"Well, when we were in 1739, we met this woman called Mrs. Hodgson. She was the one that helped us get away, and she said something strange that made us think she might not be from that time. Could she have been a *Bearer of the Medallion*?"

Grandpa Charlie frowned. "I don't know the answer to that off the top of my head. But it's certainly possible."

Bearer of the Medallion. It sounded so *serious*. "Ok," I said finally. "But it wasn't passed down to me by you. I just *found* it when we were on vacation in Miami. You aren't even-" I stopped midsentence, realizing the horrifying implications of what I was about to say.

Grandpa Charlie froze and looked up. "No. No. No matter how tempting, you must not tell me *anything* about the future. The space-time continuum is a very delicate matter. It must not be tampered with except under the most extraordinary circumstances." He continued walking. "Yes, the matter of passing on the medallion is a tricky one indeed. That's part of what I was trying to find out when Sheila – "

"What? What happened to my mother? Where is she?"

"I don't know," Grandpa Charlie answered gravely. "I was in my study, about to embark on a journey to ancient Egypt – when suddenly she burst in and grabbed the medallion at the very last second. Then, before I knew what was happening, she was gone." He looked directly at me and knelt down, holding my shoulders and looking into my eyes. "Janie, I don't know where your mother is. When I saw you, I assumed you were her, and that somehow she had managed to come back. But the medallion can only be used by or with the Bearers themselves. If Sheila's stuck back in ancient Egypt, she won't be able to use the medallion to come home!"

I stopped walking as the implications of what Grandpa Charlie was saying sank in. *She can't come home by herself, but we can go back and get her.*

Grandpa Charlie continued. "You mentioned that you tried to get home but ended up here instead. The medallion works in mysterious ways. I don't understand them all. Maybe it brought you here to save your mother!"

I shuddered, imagining my mom – or rather, a girl named Sheila who was a lot like me – stuck somewhere in ancient Egypt, alone and scared out of her mind. I glanced over at Sheila and she stared back at me, looking frightened for the first time since this whole thing had started. We had no time to lose.

******

As we headed back to Marcy's house, I remembered something.

"Uh, Grandpa, there's something else we need to do. There's going to be a horrible plane crash tomorrow - "

"Stop!" he cut me off, a wild look in his eyes. "You mustn't tell me *anything* about the future! Later, after we get your mom back, I'll explain more about the medallion and the rules we must abide by. But for now, let me make one thing clear: Interfering in the future is a very dangerous business! The tiniest little change can alter reality irreparably. Terrible things have happened when Bearers have had the hubris to believe they can engineer history!"

"What's hubris?" Sheila interrupted. That's one good thing about Sheila – she's never embarrassed to admit she doesn't know something. Her mom is always saying there's no such thing as a stupid question.

"Hubris means false pride," Grandpa explained. "Arrogance. Like when someone thinks they can do impossible things, and ends up just getting into trouble. It's important to believe in yourself, but hubris can be dangerous."

"But cousin Emma – "I stammered. "She's going to -"

"Enough! Whatever happened in your past is going to happen in our future. That's just the way the world works." But he was looking at me strangely. "Emma," he murmured softly. He was silent for several seconds before saying, "She's supposed to be flying home from New York tonight."

I felt a chill go up my spine.

"You said the space-time continuum shouldn't be tampered with *except in extraordinary circumstances*," Sheila broke in. "Aren't these extraordinary circumstances? Maybe we can't prevent the plane crash altogether, but we can try and make it so that Emma doesn't get on the plane!" She looked at Grandpa expectantly. "Maybe the medallion didn't bring us here just to save Janie's mom," she added. "Maybe it brought us here so we could save Emma too!" That's another good thing about Sheila

– she's a very good arguer. Her dad always says she'll probably become a lawyer when she grows up.

"I don't know..." Grandpa's voice trailed off. "Maybe." He looked at his watch again, and I wondered vaguely why everyone in 1985 seemed to wear watches. Maybe it was because they didn't have cell phones and stuff. "Emma told me her flight is supposed to take off tonight, shortly after midnight," he continued. "You shouldn't have told me, but now that I know... I'll see what I can do. Meanwhile, you girls have to go back and get your mom. Get the medallion to take you to May 31, 1279 BC, the day Ramses the Great ascended the throne."

"But how do we make sure to end up where my mom is?" I asked. "I mean, we tell the medallion the date we want to visit, but not the place."

"You just need to worry about *when* you want to go," Grandpa answered. "The medallion will take care of the *where*."

******

We arrived back at Marcy's house just as they were finishing supper. "My mom said it was ok for you to stay over," Marcy said as she opened the door. "Come on, let's go up to my room."

102

As we walked up the stairs, I thought about everything that had happened that day. If someone had told me I'd be traveling through time with Sheila and hanging out with my mom's eleven year old best friend, I'd have said they were stark raving mad. I'm not a very brave person. I mean, I'm not a scaredy cat or anything, but I don't even go on roller coasters at the amusement park! They make me want to throw up. The last time we went to King's Dominion, Sheila went on all the rides, even the Anaconda and the Berserker. I was too chicken.

Marcy sat on her bed, eyes wide, as Sheila filled her in on what Grandpa Charlie had told us. As she was talking, I pulled the medallion out of my pocket and turned it over in my hands.

Posei: Kudm jenkjdy osm loy jki moji a fosj ju xelej jkzii jetil. Or in plain old English: **Janie: hold tightly and say the date u want to visit three times.**

I shuddered. *Bearer of the Medallion indeed.*

"So do we all go back together?" Marcy finally said, when Sheila had finished. "I mean, she may be your mom and all, but she *is* my best friend."

I shrugged my shoulders. "I don't know. I don't see why not."

"Yeah!" Sheila said, jumping up. "Let's all go! I think we're better off sticking together. And you're really good at solving problems," she added, looking at Marcy.

I felt a fluttering in my stomach as I stretched out my hands and held the medallion up in front of me. Sheila and Marcy reached out and grasped it as well. I closed my eyes as tightly as I could. "May 31, 1279 BC! May 31, 1279 BC! May 31, 1279 BC!"

******

♥ March 21, 2011 ♥

Dear Diary,

OMG I seriously hate Mondays. First of all, it's the day we have to go back to school after the weekend. Not that I mind school that much, but still – weekends are much more fun. Second, we usually have more homework due on Mondays. I guess Mrs. Santini figures we have plenty of time to do homework over the weekend, which if you think about it, doesn't really make sense. And third, on Mondays I have piano lessons. I don't think I've told you that yet. My mom said that if I didn't take ballet, I had to take *something*, and I chose piano. I guess I don't actually hate it, but it's kind of a pain.

Yesterday I wrote so much that my hand almost fell off. But I still didn't get to the end of the story! I'm going to finish it today no matter what. So here goes...

******

We screamed as we felt ourselves falling, plunged back into the dark tunnel. I was vaguely aware of squeezing Marcy and Sheila's hands as hard as I could and yelling at the top of my lungs. And just when I thought I couldn't take even one more second-

Thud. We landed abruptly on what felt like a cold, marble floor. I opened my eyes, blinking to try and see where we were, but it was pitch black. I rubbed them and tried again. Nothing.

"Oh my gosh!" I heard Marcy exclaim. "What the -" She stopped midsentence. "I can't see anything! Can you guys see anything?"

"No," I answered, a knot of fear in my stomach. "This didn't happen last time. Last time we landed on a field in the middle of nowhere – and then in my mom's old clubhouse."

"Wait!" Sheila said suddenly, I think I see some light over there!"

I looked around me, trying to see what she was talking about. And sure enough, a tiny crack of light seemed to appear several feet away.

"I see it!" I cried excitedly. "Look, Marcy!"

We made our way carefully towards the light, and as we reached it I realized it was a tiny opening between two large, stone doors. Sheila reached out and gave one of them a gentle push. Sure enough, it swung open, and we were suddenly flooded with light.

And sound. And music. And –

I looked around, rubbed my eyes again and did a double take. The doors had opened up onto a beautiful, well-lit room, filled with tables of sumptuous food and dozens of people. In the far corner, on what seemed like a raised platform, sat a man in ancient Egyptian dress, holding what looked like a scepter. This is going to sound crazy, but it looked just like a scene from *Prince of Egypt*. As we stood there, frozen in shock, the room suddenly became completely silent. All eyes were on us.

A man standing in front of the doors began to talk excitedly, gesturing in our direction and bowing towards the figure on the raised platform. He was wearing a wrap-around skirt that was belted at the waist, and a striped, cloth headdress. He held a stick, which he was waving around in the air.

And this is the really freaky part. Even though he was speaking a foreign language, *I could understand almost everything he said!*

I looked at Sheila and Marcy, who were both frozen in place, watching him with their mouths open. If I hadn't been so scared, I probably would have burst into laughter.

"How dare you stand erect before the Pharaoh!" he was shouting, "All who come before him must bow!" He raised his stick threateningly and began walking towards us. The room filled with nervous chatter, and I took a step backwards.

"Wait!" The man on the raised platform stood, and the noise died down just as quickly as it had begun. "Look how they're dressed! They don't look like ordinary people. And see what she's holding!" He pointed his scepter in my direction. "It's a large coin, just like the one the Goddess brought us yesterday!" He reached into his tunic and pulled out a medallion. As he held it up in the air, the crowd began to chatter again.

A medallion! He had a medallion that looked just like mine!

As I stared at him, he reached out his hand as if to accept a gift. "We allow you to approach us and present us with your offering," he intoned.

Before I could say anything, Sheila grabbed my arm and pulled me back in the direction of the stone doors. "Come on guys," she whispered urgently. "We gotta get out of here. If he takes the medallion, we're finished."

******

We ran as fast as we could, not even stopping when we heard the doors slam behind us. It was pitch black again, and we had no idea where we were going. I'm not a very good runner. In gym class, I'm always one of the last people to be picked for a team (right before Ben White), and when we did the mile run, I walked most of the way. But now I ran as if my life depended on it.

"Wait!" Marcy called out, stopping and leaning forward with her hands on her knees. "I have asthma," she managed between breaths, "and I didn't bring my inhaler!"

I cast a worried glance at Sheila, but she grinned at me and started feeling around in her pockets. Eventually she pulled out a small, white inhaler. "I have asthma too," she said, handing the inhaler to Marcy. "You guys probably don't have Symbicort yet, but it works pretty well. Here, you just turn this little red thing on the bottom, and take it like a regular Ventolin puff."

Marcy accepted the inhaler and took a puff, handing it gratefully back to Sheila. "More proof you're from the future," she smiled, breathing more normally now. "As if I still needed it."

We all laughed, and it suddenly struck me that we weren't in total darkness anymore. I looked around, trying to figure out where the light was coming from, and noticed a small hole, just big enough to put my hand through, in the rock about three feet away. I walked towards it, peeking through in hopes of seeing what was on the other side. And what I saw nearly gave me a heart attack.

******

"Sh-sh-sh-sheila," I whispered loudly, beckoning for them to come over to me. "M-m-marcy, look!" I was so dumbstruck, I could barely speak.

On the other side of the wall sat a young girl, about our age, with a head of frizzy, brown hair tied up in a scrunchie. She seemed tired and haggard and looked as if she had been crying. Her jeans were torn, and she was wearing a pink tee-shirt that had WHAM written across the front in large, purple letters.

I stood back to let them look through the hole.

"Oh. My. Goodness." Marcy went white as a ghost. "It's Sheila! We've found her!"

My mom, eleven years old, was sitting on the other side of a stone wall, in a tunnel in ancient Egypt.

I must have fainted, because the next thing I knew, I was lying on the floor with my feet up, and Sheila was gently slapping my face.

"Janie, wake up!" she whispered urgently. "We've found your mother, and now we need to go home!"

I stood up shakily and peered through the hole again. The girl, hearing the commotion, had stood up and walked towards the wall.

"Hello?" she said, her voice incredulous. "Is somebody out there speaking English?"

"Sheila, it's me, Marcy! Reach out to me and hold my hand. We're gonna get you out of here!"

A sob came from the other side of the wall, and I realized my mom was crying again. "Oh, Marcy, thank goodness! They locked me up in here, and I thought I'd never get home. Oh, thank you!" I saw her hand reach out from the hole, and Marcy grasped onto it, holding it tightly.

Just then, I heard the faint sound of a man's voice echoing throughout the tunnel, speaking that strange foreign language. "They must have gone this way. There isn't any other way out of here!"

"Hurry!" I shouted, suddenly knowing exactly what needed to be done. "Grab onto the medallion!" I held it at the entrance to the hole, and waited until we were all holding onto it: Marcy, Sheila, my mother, and me. "June 22nd, 1985! June 22nd, 1985! June 22nd, 1985!"

******

This time I noticed the clubhouse didn't look anything like *my* clubhouse. First, the walls were – yup, you guessed it – pink. Ugh. Second, the posters were completely different. My J-Lo was gone, replaced with another Madonna, and an entire wall was covered with little pictures of really cute stuffed animals that said on them "Gotta Getta Gund" and looked as if they had been cut out of a magazine.

My mom stood up and brushed herself off, staring at me the entire time.

"Who are you?" she asked suspiciously. "Marcy, who are these people?"

Marcy looked at me and then at Sheila, stifling a laugh. "Well, you're not going to believe this, Sheila, but this is your daughter Janie, and her best friend Sheila."

I thought my mom's eyes were going to pop out of her head. They swept over me, inspecting my hair, my clothes and my shoes. Finally she spoke.

"This is incredibly weird. You look so much like me! If I hadn't just, uh, gotten back from ancient Egypt, I'd definitely think you were insane."

"Yeah," I smiled at her. "Me too." I was impressed by her calm, though. I'd had a whole lot more time to get used to the idea, and I was still freaking out.

"Your clothes are interesting. Not too different, but not the same, you know?"

Marcy put her hand on my mom's shoulder and grinned. "That's nothing. Wait until Sheila shows you her ipod."

"Her i-what?" My mom looked confused.

"Never mind," I said, laughing. You'll have enough time to get used to those in the future."

I bent over to tie my shoe, when the door to the clubhouse swung open, and Grandpa Charlie burst in.

"Oh, Sheila!" He ran over and gave her a huge hug, laughing and crying all at the same time. "Sheila! I was worried sick!" He stood back and looked at her, his face taking on a stern expression. "I still can't believe you did that. You're grounded, young lady! For ten days at least. And there will be absolutely no phone privileges for at least a week."

I grinned from ear to ear and pinched myself to keep from laughing. Seeing my mom get grounded – now *that* was interesting.

******

Grandpa Charlie sat across from me in my mother's room, as the story came tumbling out. "What are you going to do about your medallion?" I asked when I was done. "That Pharaoh guy in Egypt has it, and I don't think he's going to give it back anytime soon."

"That Pharaoh guy?" Grandpa repeated, raising an eyebrow in amusement. "You mean Ramses?"

"Uh, yeah." I flushed. I was nothing if not *articulate*.

"Honestly, I don't know. The important thing is that the medallion was successfully passed on to you. I don't think I need it anymore. And I think your mother has had enough adventure for the time being."

I giggled. I don't think I'll ever get used to thinking of my mom as a kid.

"Janie, you are now the only remaining Bearer of the Medallion. Being a Bearer carries a lot of responsibility." He reached over and handed me a folded piece of paper. "Read this when you get home," he said. He gave me a hug and kissed me on the cheek. "I love you, Janie. You're a wonderful kid. I'm proud of you, and I'm extremely proud of your mother for having raised a beautiful human being like yourself."

I flushed again and hugged him back, stuffing the note into my pocket. "I love you too, Grandpa."

******

Sheila and I made it back home in time for dinner that night. We were exhausted, but as far as anyone else knew, we had just been out in the clubhouse talking for a couple of hours. We came inside and I ran my hand along the back of our cream leather sofa. *Home.*

As we walked into the kitchen to make ourselves a snack, the phone rang.

"I'll get it!" SRJ jumped up and ran to the phone, grabbing it just before my mom got there.

"Oh, hello Emma," he said, handing the phone to my mom and scampering back to the living room. "It's for you, Mommy."

My mouth dropped open and I looked at Sheila. We grinned at each other. *Emma was alive!*

That night, I sat down at my computer and did a Google search for "plane crash 1985", hoping against hope not to find anything. But sure enough, the search brought up a Wikipedia entry. The crash had not been prevented. Mysteriously, the police had received an anonymous tip the night before, warning them of the disaster to come. But the future was resistant to change.

******

♥ March 22, 2011 ♥

Dear Diary,

So I finally finished telling you the story. But it isn't really over, is it? Sheila's coming over after school tomorrow to read the note from Grandpa Charlie with me, and we have a lot to talk about. I'm dying to know what's in it, but I don't want to read it myself.

Things with Mom have been better than usual. Somehow, when I look at her, I can't help seeing the little kid she used to be. The messy slob whose (pink!) room looked like it had been hit by a hurricane. The uncertain girl who worried her best friend would be snatched away from her, and who got bad grades in math and hated ballet. She's still on my case all the time to clean my room, brush my hair and do my homework – but something is different.

Like yesterday after school, when I was complaining I was bored, and she told me for the one millionth time that I should consider taking ballet. I looked at her and asked, "Did you like ballet when you were my age, Mom?" Usually, she just would have given me an exasperated look and told me a story about what a swell experience it was. But yesterday she just gave me a little smile, winked and said, "Well you know, my friend Marcy and I just *loved* it."

I <u>really</u> have to talk to Sheila.

TO BE CONTINUED...

****

The Diary of Janie Ray:

The Impossible Medallion

The Day My Mom Got Grounded

A Star is Born

A Letter to My Fifth Grade Self

Baking with Frenemies!

The Case of the Missing Medallion

And look out for Book 7 of The Diary of Janie Ray, coming soon!

CPSIA information can be obtained
at www.ICGtesting.com
Printed in the USA
BVOW06s0236211217
503370BV00022B/1249/P